D1026788

POLAR BEARS ON ICE

To all my teammates
on the *Lady Lightning*
—K.F.

Library and Archives Canada Cataloguing in Publication

Flanagan, Kate
Polar Bears on ice / written and illustrated by Kate Flanagan.
(Scholastic reader level 2)

ISBN 978-0-545-98599-4

I. Title. II. Series: Scholastic reader. Level 2

PZ7.F59829Po 2009   j813'.6   C2009-903429-8

ISBN-10 0-545-98599-4

6 5 4 3 2 1   Printed in Canada   09 10 11 12 13

Mixed Sources
Product group from well-managed
forests and other controlled sources
www.fsc.org Cert no. SGS-COC-003098
© 1996 Forest Stewardship Council
FSC

POLAR BEARS ON ICE

KATE FLANAGAN

SCHOLASTIC CANADA LTD.
New York Toronto London Auckland Sydney
Mexico City New Delhi Hong Kong Buenos Aires

Maggie flew across the ice
in her white skates.

She jumped.

She twirled.

She spun.

She zipped circles around
her teacher, Mrs. Crump.

She crashed and banged
and slid on the ice.

"Be graceful, Maggie!"
Mrs. Crump shouted.
"Glide like a swan!"

Maggie tried.
But sometimes she didn't feel
like a graceful swan.
"Look at me, Mrs. Crump! I'm
a kangaroo! Boing, boing, boing!"

"Maggie has such spirit," Mrs.
Crump said, shaking her head.
"If only she would learn to listen!"

One day Maggie was at
the skating rink early.
Some kids with polar bears
on their shirts were playing hockey.

They zipped up the ice.
They zipped down the ice.
They crashed and banged
and whacked.

Maggie put her face up against
the glass and watched.
There were no graceful swans
on the ice.

"*Grrrrrrrrr!*" Maggie said
to her mother. "I want
to do that!"

Nobody could change Maggie's mind.
Not her mother.

Not her father.

Not even Mrs. Crump.

Soon the white skates
were packed away.
Maggie got new skates.
And a helmet, a stick, gloves,
and a blue shirt with a polar bear
on it.
"Grrrrrr!" she said.

Every week Maggie skated
with her new team.
When Coach Mike blew his whistle,
everyone listened—even Maggie.

They skated up and down,
forward and backward.
They practiced starts and stops
and turns.

Sometimes Maggie couldn't help adding an extra jump.

Or spin.

Or twirl.

The other Polar Bears fell down
laughing when they saw her.

"Maggie, are you a bear or a ballerina?"
coach Mike asked.
Maggie just growled as she twirled
away.

The team got better and better.
Coach Mike had some news
for them.

"Our first game will be
against the Huntsville Huskies."
Everybody was quiet.
The Huskies were the best
team around.

"They're a good team," Coach Mike said, "but I think we can beat them!" The Polar Bears cheered.

Maggie leaped onto the ice
and landed in a spin.
She couldn't wait
to face the Huskies.

The stands were full
on the day of the game.
Maggie waved to her parents
as she skated onto the ice.

The Huntsville Huskies
were warming up.
They looked big and mean.

Coach Mike gave the Polar Bears
a pep talk.
"Keep your heads up and
your feet moving. Play hard
and you'll do fine!"
The Polar Bears put their hands
together and cheered.

The game began.
Blue shirts and gold shirts raced
back and forth across the rink.
The crowd cheered.

Today Maggie felt like a bear.
She crashed.
She banged.
She growled.
She never had so much fun.

With ten seconds left in the game,
Coach Mike called a time out.
The score was tied, 2–2.
"We only have time for one shot,"
he said. "I need my best skater
out there."
He looked at Maggie.
"How do you feel?" he asked.
"Like a Polar Bear!" she shouted.

"Go get 'em!" Coach Mike said.
Maggie jumped onto the ice.

She heard the crowd cheer.
The ref dropped the puck.

Bang! It sailed toward Maggie.
She caught it on her stick
and turned up the ice.

A Huskie poked his stick at her.
She jumped.

A gold shirt raced toward her.
She spun.

Only one Huskie was left.
Maggie twirled.

With a flick of her stick,
she popped the puck
toward the goal.
She scored!

The buzzer rang.
The Polar Bears jumped
all over Maggie.
"We won! We won!"
they shouted.
Everyone fell in a heap
on the ice.

"That's my girl!" a voice said.
"Graceful as a swan!"

Maggie peeked out from under
the pile at Mrs. Crump.
"*Grrrrrr!*" Maggie said.
"I'm a Polar Bear now."

Mrs. Crump pulled Maggie
to her feet and hugged her.
"A graceful Polar Bear,"
Mrs. Crump said.
Maggie smiled.